# Ronnie's Treasure Hunt

by Pippa Goodhart
illustrated by Deborah Allwright

PICTURE WINDOW BOOKS
Minneapolis, Minnesota

*For my nephew, David Goodhart, with love*

Editor: Shelly Lyons
Page Production: Melissa Kes
Art Director: Nathan Gassman
Associate Managing Editor: Christianne Jones

First American edition published in 2009 by
Picture Window Books
151 Good Counsel Drive
P.O. Box 669
Mankato, MN 56002-0669
1-877-845-8392
www.picturewindowbooks.com

First published in 2006 by A & C Black Publishers, Ltd,
38 Soho Square, London W1D 3HB www.acblack.com
Text copyright © 2006 Pippa Goodhart
Illustrations copyright © 2006 Deborah Allwright

Printed in the United States of America.

All books published by Picture Window Books
are manufactured with paper containing at least
10 percent post-consumer waste.

Library of Congress Cataloging-in-Publication Data
Goodhart, Pippa.
Ronnie's treasure hunt / written by Pippa Goodhart ; illustrated by
Deborah Allwright.
p. cm. — (Read-it! chapter books)
ISBN-13: 978-1-4048-4905-1 (library binding)
I. Allwright, Deborah, ill. II. Title.
PZ7.G6125Ron 2008
[E]—dc22                                          2008007780

# Table of Contents

# Chapter One

"I'm bored," said Ronnie. He kicked the table, and a box of cookies fell to the floor.

"Now look what you have done!" said his mom. "I'm trying to clean up, and you are making a mess!"

"Sorry," said Ronnie.

"And I'm a mess, too," said his mom, sadly.

6

"Everything is a mess!"

"Don't worry," said Ronnie. "It's your
birthday tomorrow. That will cheer you up."

But he hadn't bought her a present yet.
What could he get to make her happy?

Ronnie shook his piggy bank. It was empty.

He checked his pockets. He found one sticky old piece of candy.

So, he set off down the road, looking for things. He saw some flowers, but they weren't pretty—they were weeds.

He saw something shiny, but it wasn't jewels or gold—it was a puddle.

Then he saw a rocket parked by the side of
the road.

"Wow!" said Ronnie. "Whose is that?"

"IT'S OURS! HA-HA!" yelled a pirate.

# Chapter Two

"Pirates!" said Ronnie. "What are you doing on my road?"

"Ha-ha!" yelled the captain. "We're looking for treasure."

"Well, there isn't any treasure here," said Ronnie. "I have already looked."

"Ah, but we're hunting for treasure from the skies!" said the captain.

Ronnie looked up at the cloudy sky. "What treasure?" he asked. "There's no treasure way up there."

"It's *hidden* treasure, boy! Hidden until nighttime, when it puts on a show," answered the captain. "Have you never looked out of a window at night and seen treasures sparkling in the sky?"

"No," said Ronnie.

"You mean you have never seen that fat, round opal they call the moon?" roared the captain. "You have never seen those diamonds up there, scattered in the sky?"

"Those aren't diamonds," said Ronnie. "They're stars."

"Call them what you like," said the captain.
"I intend to have those twinklers just as soon
as we have ourselves a cabin boy for our
rocket. Grab the boy, Dolly! Tie him up, Shanks!"
"But my mom—" Ronnie began.

Before Ronnie could finish what he was saying, Shanks gagged him. Then the pirate carried him into the rocket and shut the door. "Mmph, bmph, wmph!" mumbled Ronnie. "Quiet, boy! We're off into space!" yelled Shanks.

"Countdown!" ordered the captain. "Ten, nine, seven, two, three, liftoff!"

Nothing happened.

"What's wrong with this goofy rocket?" roared the captain.

23

"Untie the boy, and let's hear what he has to say!" said the captain.

"You have counted wrong," said Ronnie. "This is how you count."

# Chapter Three

Ronnie and the pirates shot through the clouds and up into the clear sky above. Then everything was silent. There was nothing twinkling in space that Ronnie could see, except the blazing orange fire of the sun.

"We're not going to try and catch the sun, are we?" asked Ronnie.

"Of course not!" said the captain. "We're not stupid. That old sun is too hot to touch. We're only after twinklers we can handle. And we must be ready to grab them quickly when everything goes dark. Mr. Shanks, get out the grabber and polish her up. Boy, you can mend the hole in the booty bag."

They all got busy, and soon it grew dark.
Space was spotted with stars and planets.

The captain rubbed his hands together
and said, "See? There's lots and lots of
lovely treasure!"

"That's the best one!" said Shanks, pointing toward the biggest, shiniest star.

"It's only a rock with the sun shining on it," said Ronnie.

But nobody listened to him.

"Steer moon-starboard, Mr. Shanks,"
ordered the captain. He held up a finger.
"See that twinkler? It will fit nicely in a ring."
The nearer they got to the twinkler, the
bigger and bigger it grew.

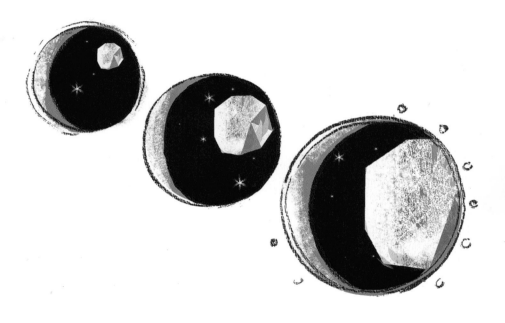

"What a whopper!" said the captain. "Dolly,
cook up something to give us strength for
grabbing. Boy, you can peel the carrots."

Dolly put sausages, carrots, peas, and potatoes into a pot. Then she threw in a pair of dirty socks.

"What are you doing?" asked Ronnie.

"I'm washing the captain's socks," said Dolly. "There's no point in wasting hot water. Don't worry. I'll take them out before I serve you all."

The smell from the pot was terrible.
"I'm not eating that!" said Ronnie.
"Yes, you are!" said Dolly.
"No, I'm not!" yelled Ronnie.

The pirates were so busy arguing that they
didn't notice they had reached the big twinkler
until they hit it.

# Chapter Four

"Everybody out!" said the captain. "Bring the grabber and the booty bag!"

He opened the door, and they all climbed out. Then they stopped.

They were standing on dark, dusty rocks.
Nothing was twinkling.

"Oh," said the captain.

"Er," said Shanks.

"Um," said Dolly.

"I told you it wasn't a real diamond," said Ronnie.

But the captain was pointing at something. "W-w-what's that?" he stammered.

"Just a little alien," said Ronnie.

"Help!" roared the captain. "It will eat us alive! Get back to the rocket. Quick!"

Shanks, Dolly, and the captain ran.

Ronnie was watching the alien. It was
sucking up dust and rocks, and it was smiling.
*That's a strange diet*, thought Ronnie.

Ronnie bent down to pet the alien. It was soft. "Hello," he said.

"Burble, blip," said the alien. It rested its head on Ronnie's lap and looked up at him.

"I like you!" said Ronnie. "My mom would like you, too. You could help clean up our messy house. Would you like to come home with me?"

"Bloodle, bess!" said the alien as it wagged all of its tails.

Ronnie slipped the alien into the booty bag and climbed back into the rocket. The engines roared, and the crew began the countdown.

There was a great rush of rocket noise, and they swooped into space.

# Chapter Five

Ronnie saw Earth getting bigger and bigger.
It was blue, green, and white. It was beautiful.

Ronnie let the alien peek out of the bag.

"That's where we're going," Ronnie whispered. "That's home."

"Zing, ping!" said the alien.

"What did you say, boy?" asked the captain.

"Er, I said, perhaps we should sing," said Ronnie, stuffing the alien back into the bag.

"Sing?" asked the captain.

"Yes, sing 'Happy Birthday' to my mom," said Ronnie. "Today is her birthday, and you're all invited to my house for a party."

"I like parties!" said Shanks.

"We'll need to bring a present," said Dolly.

"I have my mom's birthday present here," said Ronnie.

"What—" began the captain. But he didn't have time to say any more because …

The rocket landed, back on Ronnie's road.

"Look at that!" said Shanks as he and the others climbed out of the rocket.

Everything on Earth was beautiful in the moonlight. Even the weeds looked pretty, so Ronnie picked some.

When Ronnie's mom opened the door and stepped outside, she looked lovely, too.

"Ronnie! Where on Earth have you been?" she asked.

"I haven't been on Earth, Mom," said Ronnie.

"I've been in space! And I've brought you some presents. Look!"

Ronnie held out the flowers, and then he pulled the little alien from the bag.

"How lovely! It's just what I need," said Ronnie's mom.

But Ronnie's mom was looking at the
captain. He was gazing back at her.

"Would you look at that!" said the captain.
"Just look at your mom's eyes, Ronnie. I reckon
I've found my twinklers after all."
Everyone was happy.

# Look for More
## *Read-It!*
# Chapter Books

Alice Goes North
The Badcat Gang
Beastly Basil
Cat Baby
Cleaner Genie
Clever Monkeys
Contest Crazy
Disgusting Denzil
Elvis the Squirrel

Eye, Eye, Captain!
High Five Hank
Hot Dog and the Talent Competition
Mr. Croc Rocks
On the Ghost Trail
Sid and Bolter
Stan the Dog Becomes Superdog
The Thing in the Basement
Tough Ronald

## On the Web

FactHound offers a safe, fun way to find Web sites related to topics in this book. All of the sites on FactHound have been researched by our staff.

1. Visit *www.facthound.com*

2. Type in this special code:
   140484905X

3. Click on the FETCH IT button.

Your trusty FactHound will fetch the best sites for you!

Looking for a specific title or level? A complete list of
*Read-it!* Chapter Books is available on our Web site:
**www.picturewindowbooks.com**